Eddie Spaghetti
on the Home Front

EDDIE SPAGHETTI ON THE HOMEFRONT

★

Edward Frascino

★

HARPER & ROW, PUBLISHERS

NEW YORK

Cambridge London
Hagerstown   Mexico City
Philadelphia   São Paulo
San Francisco   Sydney

1817

Library of Congress Cataloging in Publication Data
Frascino, Edward.
    Eddie Spaghetti on the home front.

    Summary: Eddie does as much as a boy can for the war
effort during World War II.
    [1. Yonkers (N.Y.)—Fiction.   2. World War, 1939–
1945—Fiction]   I. Title.
PZ7.F8596Eg 1983   [Fic]   82-48847
ISBN 0-06-021894-0
ISBN 0-06-021895-9 (lib. bdg.)

Contents

Eddie Spaghetti
on the Home Front

★ 1 ★

Pearl Harbor

I'm at the movies with my father, my mother, and my brother Angel. The picture is *Suspicion*, and it's at Radio City Music Hall, the biggest theater in the world. The leading man and leading lady are Cary Grant and Joan Fontaine. They're married, and she suspects he has murdered Nigel Bruce. Now she's afraid he is trying to poison her. Joan Fontaine is sick in bed, and Cary Grant is bringing her a glass of milk when all of a sudden the movie stops, and the lights come on. A man walks out on Radio City Music Hall's huge stage.

"Ladies and gentlemen," he says, "we have just received a confirmed report that Japanese planes have bombed the United States military base in Pearl Harbor, Hawaii."

"We're in the war now," the man sitting behind me says to his wife.

The theater is packed and everybody is talking, and some people get up and leave.

"Are we going to war, Pa?" I ask.

"I don't know, Eddie," my father says.

3

I look at my mother. She's looking at my father but she doesn't say anything. I feel scared.

"I've got to call my sister in Los Angeles," a lady in our row says. She's bumping people's knees pushing past them toward the aisle.

"Hold your horses!" another lady says, standing up to let her by.

"They may be bombing California!" The first lady raises her voice. "I have to call my sister."

"There is no cause for alarm," the man on the stage says. "The continental United States is in no immediate danger. Please keep your seats."

He walks off the stage, the lights go out, and *Suspicion* starts again.

People are still talking. My father and mother are talking Albanèse so Angel and I won't understand what they're saying. Albanèse is the language they talk in the part of Italy that my parents come from. I can't understand the words, but from the sound of their voices I'll bet my mother is saying we should leave, and my father is saying we'll stay till the end of the movie.

Joan Fontaine was wrong about Cary Grant wanting to murder her. He really loves her, and that's The End.

"Come on," my mother says, and gets up and puts on her coat with the silver fox collar.

"Aren't we going to see the stage show, Ma?" Angel says.

"It's getting late, and Grandma is expecting us," she says. "Put your coat on."

"You'll come back with Mama to see the stage show during Christmas vacation," my father says. "O.K., big boy?"

Angel looks disappointed, but I don't mind because I'll get to see another movie in the biggest theater in the world.

When we get to Grandma's, she, my cousin Dotty, and Uncle Hugo are listening to the radio. It's all about Pearl Harbor. Six American battleships were sunk, and one hundred and sixty-four American planes were destroyed on the ground.

". . . over one thousand Americans are known dead," the newsman is saying, "but the final toll is expected to be much higher."

Grandma doesn't understand much English, so Dotty and Uncle Hugo are translating the news into Albanèse.

I look forward to Sunday at Grandma's because it's always fun, but today it's not. Everybody is serious. Angel and I just sit and look out the window. If Grandma's piano wasn't in our basement in Yonkers, I could at least play that.

Grandma is talking a lot in Albanèse. Every

6

once in a while my mother and Dotty say something to each other in English. Grandma is worried because Uncle Hugo is twenty years old and might get drafted into the Army. I'm ten, and Angel's eight, so we'll never get drafted, but I'll bet the Army is better than school.

"She won't listen," Dotty is telling my mother. "They'll never take Hugo with his eyes." Uncle Hugo wears very thick eyeglasses. He can hardly see without them.

Grandma is getting excited. My father and mother are trying to calm her down because she has heart trouble and excitement is bad for that. Grandpa died of heart trouble.

Uncle Hugo isn't saying much, just smoking one cigarette after another. He smokes Camels and gives me the empty packs for the tinfoil that's inside to keep the cigarettes fresh. I'm rolling it into a ball, until it's so huge it will be in *Ripley's Believe It or Not!* So far it's only as big as a Ping-Pong ball.

Now Dotty is getting excited. She sounds angry with Grandma. She says some things in Albanèse real loud and then takes Uncle Hugo's glasses right off his nose to show Grandma how thick the lenses are. Uncle Hugo yells at Dotty and grabs his glasses.

"Dotty," my father says, "don't get excited."

7

"I'll get excited if I want to!" Dotty raises her voice. "I don't have heart trouble."

"Dotty, what a thing to say," my mother says, and then she talks to Grandma in Albanèse.

"All right, you reason with her," Dotty says. "I'm going to do my nails." She goes into the bathroom and slams the door.

"Yesterday, December 7, 1941—a date which will live in infamy—" President Roosevelt says on the radio the next day, "the United States of America was suddenly and deliberately attacked by naval and air forces of the Empire of Japan."

He's asking Congress to declare war on Japan. I get the dictionary and look up "infamy." It says: "very bad reputation; notoriety; disgrace; dishonor."

★ 2 ★

Scrap Drive

It's six months since Pearl Harbor, and everything everyone does these days is for the war effort.

Squeak-creak! Squeak-creak!

"The wheels on this wagon are so rusty, I'll bet they can hear us coming a mile away," Angel says.

"Well, it comes in handy today," I say.

Our school is having a big Scrap Drive, and all us kids were given an extra hour for lunch to go around collecting empty tin cans, pieces of scrap metal, rubber, and newspapers. The government needs those things to make guns and stuff.

"I thought the wagon would be full of scrap by now," says Angel.

"Miss Graham said, 'Every little bit helps the war effort.'" Miss Graham is my teacher.

"That beat-up rubber sink stopper we found is a *real* little bit," Angel says. "It's hard pulling this wagon."

"Let me." The handle squeaks when he passes it to me. "Remember how smooth it rolled when the tires were new? Now they're worn right down to the rim."

"That's how our car wheels are going to look if the war lasts long and Pa can't get new tires," Angel says.

"Nobody can drive much anyway, with the gas rationing," I say.

We pass a house with a blue star hanging in the window. That means someone living there is in the service. All men between nineteen and forty-four are eligible to be drafted, unless they're 4-F, which means they have asthma or a punctured eardrum or flat feet or something. Uncle Hugo isn't 4-F even with his bad eyesight. Now men forty-five to sixty-five have to register for the draft. My father registered, but he says he won't be called unless we start losing the war badly.

The whole world is at war except for a few neutral countries like Switzerland. Great Britain, France, Russia, and China are some of the big countries on our side. We're the Allies. Japan, Germany, and Italy are fighting against us. They're the Axis. My father and Grandma—she's my mother's mother—were born in Italy, but they came to America before Mussolini took over.

They don't like him and were angry when he joined Hitler to conquer Europe. My mother remembers World War I, and she says this is worse.

"What about the tin cans and newspapers Ma saves?" Angel asks. "We could take those to school."

"I asked her, but yesterday was the day the garbage men collected scrap. Look! There's something shiny up ahead!" I start to run.

"Forget it." Angel sounds tired. "It's only a puddle reflecting the sun."

"I don't think an extra hour is enough," I complain. "We should have the whole afternoon. Let's try Leroy Place." We turn the corner. "Oh, no!"

There are those Egan kids who live up the block from us. Richie and Mikey are carrying a dented car fender, and their little sister Peggy has a piece of old garden hose.

"I wonder where they found the fender?" Angel says.

"Probably stole it off someone's car." I think about turning back around the corner before they see us.

"There's Eddie Spaghetti," Mikey says. He's about my size. Richie is a little bigger.

"Why don't you oil those wheels?" Richie yells at me.

11

"*Sssss!*" Peggy hisses, and wiggles the hose. "Watch out, Eddie Spaghetti. This python is going to squeeze you."

They all giggle, and my face turns red. I wish I could think of something smart to say back, but I never can.

"Hey, Mikey," Angel says, "I saw a man with only three fenders on his car. Boy, was he mad."

They all giggle again, even my brother. I feel dumb pulling this big, old, squeaky wagon with nothing in it except that stupid little sink stopper.

"Hey, Eddie Spaghetti!" Richie yells. "You gonna beat the Axis with all that scrap you collected?"

The Egan kids start walking away, singing that song they always sing to tease me:

> *Eddie Spaghetti—*
> *Put him in a pot.*
> *Turn up the fire*
> *And watch him get hot.*

I want to run, but I just try to ignore them. "Come on," I say to Angel.

He's smiling, and his dumb dimples show.

"Since when are you friends with Mikey?"

"I'm not," Angel says. "We play softball on opposite teams. There's a game tomorrow. You want to play?"

13

"I don't know."

Whenever they choose up sides to play softball at school, I'm always the last one picked. I'm a lousy hitter.

"I hate those Egan kids." I feel my face turn red again.

"Well, if you didn't act so stuck-up, maybe they wouldn't tease you."

"I'm *not* stuck-up."

"Then why don't you talk to them?"

"Why should I? I don't like them."

"Then say something rotten."

"I usually think of something too late, and by the time I see them again I forget it."

"Where should we go now?" Angel is trying to decide. "I'll bet there's plenty of scrap lying around near Jim the Hermit's shack."

"Maybe," I say, "but yesterday Dukie got in a fight with that big cat Jim has, and Jim chased us with a stick."

"I guess we should start heading back to school." Angel is ready to give up.

"Two of us with one little sink stopper?" I say. "Let's not go back. Maybe Ma will write us a note saying we got sick at lunch."

Angel looks at me as if to say there's not much chance of that.

"So we'll get the booby prize." He smiles. "I want to see what everybody else found."

*

"We should have left the wagon home," I say as we cross the street in front of P.S. 17.

"Well, we might have found something on the way," Angel says.

"Now I have to pull this dumb wagon all the way back after school."

"We'll take turns."

We walk around to the school playground where there's a big pile of all kinds of stuff. Kids are dumping their scrap on the pile and then standing around to see what other kids found. Miss Graham is there, and some other teachers, too. Everybody hears us coming. I see the Egan kids on the other side of the pile.

"We can't go squeaking all the way up to the scrap pile," I say (even my voice sounds squeaky), "just to add this stinky little stopper. Wait here."

I hand Angel the wagon handle and pick up the stopper. That's when I get this terrific idea.

"Come on, I have a better idea, Angel."

Now I'm glad we're making all this noise, because the teachers, the Egans, and everybody see us walk right up to the scrap pile. I toss the stopper on, and then I pick up the wagon and dump it on the pile, too.

"What are you . . . ?" Angel starts to say, and then he smiles. "Yeah!"

I can't help looking over at the Egans. Mikey

and Peggy are giggling. Richie has a funny look on his face.

"I gave my wagon to the Scrap Drive, Ma," I tell her when I get home after school.

"I'm glad," my mother says. "It wasn't doing anybody any good rusting in the garage."

"Come on, Dukie," I call to my dog, and we run out into the empty lot where the grass is tall. We lie on the ground, and I look straight up so all I can see is blue sky and white clouds.

"School will be over in two weeks, Duke. Then we can spend all day together."

Dukie rolls over and rests his head on my arm.

I wish I could do something for the war effort during my summer vacation. I'd really like to be in the Army. I don't have asthma, a punctured eardrum, or flat feet, and kids fought in the American Revolution, like the drummer boy in the *Spirit of '76*.

Maybe I could work in a defense plant. This magazine I saw at the barber's had pictures of midgets who work on airplanes in the small places where regular-sized people can't fit. I could do that. Grown-ups don't let kids do anything important. I'll bet I could be a spy. No one would suspect a kid of carrying military plans or having the key to a secret code. Those Egan kids would make good spies for the Axis.

"I know, Dukie. Next time I see those Egans, I'm going to say, 'Heil, Egan!' and give the Nazi salute. I hope I remember."

★ 3 ★

Jim the Hermit

"Are we going to eat soon?" I ask my mother.

"Soon enough," she answers, "and will you please take that dog out of here."

Dukie is begging for something to eat.

"Come on, Duke." I take hold of his collar and lead him out of the kitchen.

Angel is in the living room reading the funnies. I have to wait till he's finished to see what happened in *The Phantom*, *Mandrake the Magician*, and the other comic strips. Dukie jumps on Angel to say hello, and his paw tears right through *Joe Palooka*.

"Hi, Dukie," Angel says.

Dukie tries to lick his face.

"Are you almost finished?" I ask Angel.

"No."

I sit down and look at the other half of the newspaper. On the front page is a story about saboteurs who came by submarine and landed on Long Island. They had TNT and maps of de-

19

fense plants and railroad terminals. One of their targets was the Hell Gate railroad bridge from Astoria, Queens, to the Bronx (I was born in the Bronx), but thanks to the FBI all the saboteurs were arrested. Jim the Hermit's shack would be a good place for saboteurs to hide their dynamite.

When we moved to Dunwoodie Street two years ago, Jim was living in his shack five or six empty lots away from our house, which is the last house on the block. (No new houses are being built because of the war.) Jim's shack is built out of old pieces of wood, tin, and tar paper, and surrounded by trees and bushes. Now that it's summer you can hardly see it. It's spooky.

"Who is he?" I asked my friend Neil.

"He's a bank robber hiding from the police," Neil told me.

"But everyone in the neighborhood knows he's there, so the police must know, too."

"I looked in his window once," Neil said. "Jim was sitting on the floor counting lots and lots of money. About a million dollars I bet."

I wouldn't call Neil a liar to his face, but he does like to make things up.

Jim is short, thin, and old, and he lives all alone with a big, orange, tiger-striped cat that Dukie fights with.

"That hermit gives me the creeps," my mother tells people. "I always make sure the doors are locked when I'm alone in the house."

"I'm finished," Angel says, and hands me the funny page.

"Thanks," I say, but before I look at *The Phantom* I read about the saboteurs again.

My father comes into the living room. His sleeves are rolled up, and he's mopping his forehead with a red bandanna. When he gets home from work, he goes out and works in the Victory garden.

"Eddie," he says, "thanks for moving that old wagon from the garage. Did you put it someplace out of the way?"

"I gave it to the Scrap Drive at school today."

"Good boy. Papa's tired—will you do me a favor?"

"Sure, Pa."

"Go to the store for a couple of flashlight batteries? You know there's a blackout tonight."

"I know. Should I go now?"

"Mama says you have time before dinner. Here's an extra dime. You can buy a comic book."

"Thanks, Pa."

On my way to the store I have to pass the Egan

21

house. I'm ready to do "Heil, Egan!" but no-body's around. They must be eating.

I buy the batteries in the little candy store on the corner of Yonkers Avenue, and I also buy a new *Jumbo Comics*. While I'm walking home I start reading *Sheena, Queen of the Jungle*.

When I get to Dunwoodie Street, I'm so busy reading that I nearly bump right into Jim the Hermit. I stop dead in my tracks and cover my face with the comic book. I hope he doesn't recognize me from yesterday afternoon. I peek over the top of the comic book just as Jim passes. He doesn't even look at me. I've never been this close to him. He's spooky. There are lots of little wrinkles around his eyes and blue veins showing on his nose, and he hasn't shaved for a couple of days.

I wait for him to get far ahead. Boy, he walks slow. He's carrying a big pot that probably has his dinner in it. My mother says people in the neighborhood give him food. I watch him walk down Dunwoodie Street with his head bent forward. Now the Egan kids are in their front yard waiting for the Good Humor man. When they see Jim, they all run into the house. I didn't think they were scared of anything. I watch Jim pass my house and hear Dukie bark at him through the screen door. Good dog.

It's safe for me to start walking again. When I get home, Jim the Hermit is way down on the unpaved part of Dunwoodie Street where Dukie and I play. He turns and climbs the slope toward his shack.

★ 4 ★

Blackout

"What are you doing?" my mother yells upstairs.

"Filling the bathtub!" I yell back.

"What for?" she yells. "We're going to eat soon!"

"For the blackout tonight!" I yell.

The running water is making it hard to hear, so I come out of the bathroom and walk halfway down the stairs. My mother is standing at the foot of the stairs.

"Ma, do we have any buckets?"

"What are you going to do with buckets?"

"Fill them with water, and the big spaghetti pot could be filled, too."

"Eddie, I'm using the spaghetti pot. Why are you doing this now? Dinner is almost on the table."

"O.K.," and I start downstairs.

"Wait a minute. Are you going to leave the water running until it overflows?"

I run back to the bathroom and turn off the water.

"Mario! Angel!" My mother is calling my father and my brother. "Come and eat."

Today is Thursday. We have spaghetti Sundays and Thursdays, but because of the war we can't buy canned tomatoes, cheese, and olive oil from Italy anymore. The tomatoes, cheese, and oil we get now don't taste as good. We could buy the imported stuff from the black market, but that's against the law and unpatriotic, and besides, it's expensive.

"I'm not going to make those gangsters rich," my father said.

Dukie is eating in the kitchen. I guess dog food doesn't taste any different because of the war. He gobbles it up as fast as ever and then comes to beg from the table.

"What time is the blackout?" Angel says.

"Nine thirty," my father says. "Are we ready?"

"Ask your other son," my mother says. "He filled the bathtub, and now he wants to fill my pots and pans."

"Why?" My father looks at me.

"In an air raid," I explain, "you're supposed to be prepared to put out fires. In case a bomb hits your house. I read it in the paper."

"And how much time do you think you're going to have to fill the tub in a real air raid?" my mother says.

"If a bomb hits our house," Angel says, "we'll be in little pieces all over Dunwoodie Street."

My mother puts down her fork and says, "Angel, please! We're eating."

"We'd be safe in the basement," I tell them, "sitting under a heavy table."

"There's only that rickety old card table down there," Angel says.

"This is just practice." My father's voice is comforting. "We couldn't have a real air raid. There's radar all along the coastline. It would pick up any enemy bombers in plenty of time for our fighter planes to shoot them down."

My mother says something in Albanèse to my father.

"The sauce is good, Rose," he says. "Eat."

After dinner we're all in the living room listening to *Baby Snooks* on the radio. The phone rings, and my mother goes to answer it. After she says, "Hello," she starts talking Albanèse, so it must be Grandma.

"Mario," my mother calls, "Mama wants to talk to you."

My father goes to the phone to talk to Grandma.

My mother comes back into the living room.

"Your Uncle Hugo got his draft notice today." She looks very serious.

"Is he going into the Army?" Angel asks. "I'd rather be in the Navy."

"Probably the Army." My mother sighs. "That's where they put most of the boys."

"Pa says he'll get a desk job." I hope I sound comforting.

"I know." My mother nods.

My father comes into the living room and puts his arm around my mother's shoulders. She looks as if she's going to cry.

"Rose," he says, "why don't you cut four nice big pieces of your apple pie and put four big scoops of vanilla ice cream on top, and we'll go downstairs and have a blackout party."

"All right," my mother says, and she goes to the kitchen.

"Angel," my father says, "go down to the playroom like a big boy and close all the curtains so no light can get out."

"O.K.," Angel says, and Dukie follows him down to the basement.

My mother made blackout curtains just for the playroom windows. All the lights upstairs will be turned off. We only light one candle in the playroom during a blackout because even with the curtains, electric light shines through.

"Pa, I'm going upstairs to finish filling the tub," I say.

"O.K., but as soon as you hear the air raid siren, I want you in the playroom."

"O.K.," and I run upstairs.

I look at the clock in my room. It's almost nine thirty. I hurry to the bathroom and turn on both faucets in the tub full blast.

The only people allowed outside during a blackout are the air raid wardens. They wear white helmets with AIR RAID WARDEN printed on them and walk around to make sure no lights are showing. I read that even a lighted match can be seen from a bomber way up in the sky. I wish I could be an air raid warden. My father was going to, but the idea upset my mother, so he didn't.

Weeoow! Weeoow! Weeoow! Weeoow!

The air raid siren.

I turn off the bathroom light. All the other lights upstairs are off.

"Eddie!" my father calls. "Come on!"

"Coming!" I yell.

I just want to see the streetlights go out. The bathroom window faces empty lots, but past the lots, way over on a hill, are houses and street-lights.

Everything on the hill is pitch black now. I start to go, but I see this light blinking in a clump of trees. It stops, and everything's dark. Then

29

it starts again. It looks like a signal. I know what's in that clump of trees—Jim the Hermit's shack!

"Eddie! Your ice cream is melting." My mother sounds mad.

I start to go and remember the bathtub. I turn off the water just before it's about to overflow.

I feel my way along the wall and down to the first floor, where I bump into my mother.

"Where were you?" she says. "Do you think I like stumbling around in the dark looking for you?"

"I saw a light, Ma. Out in the empty lot."

"The air raid warden will take care of it."

"But it was blinking. Like a signal."

"A signal? What next?" She taps my shoulder. "Come on, move."

"It could be a spy," I say, "signaling the bombers."

"There are no bombers," my mother says. "This is just practice."

I think a moment and say, "Well, maybe the spy is practicing, too. Maybe the Nazis are planning a real air raid, and the spy is going to show them where to drop the bombs."

"And what happens to the spy in a real air raid—when the bombs fall?" My mother is losing her patience.

"He could be on a suicide mission," I say.

"Where did you get that idea? From the movies, I suppose. Come on. Downstairs."

Candlelight makes the playroom look like a haunted house. I should have put a sheet over my head and come down pretending to be a ghost. I'll bet I would have scared everyone except Dukie.

I eat my apple pie in vanilla ice cream gravy. That's the way I like it. I wonder if Jim the Hermit could be a spy?

★ 5 ★

The Defense Club

Dukie runs alongside trying to grab the cuff of my pants. He's having fun. I think he knows it's the first day of my summer vacation. We make a wide detour around Jim the Hermit's shack. I'll bet the air raid warden didn't even check it during the blackout two weeks ago. It's scary to think about sneaking close enough to see if Jim has an aerial on his roof for a shortwave radio. If I could be brave enough and saw anything suspicious, I'd tell the FBI. That would really be doing something for the war effort.

"Come on, Duke!"

We run through tall grass and trees toward the clubhouse. One weekend when Uncle Hugo visited, he built it for Angel and me. I wanted a tree house like Tarzan's, but Uncle Hugo said the wooden crates he was using weren't strong enough, so he built it under a tree.

In front of the clubhouse Angel and I started digging a moat like they had around the castle in *Robin Hood*. So far we've only dug about a foot deep and two feet wide. I don't know when it'll be finished. We left the shovel in the clubhouse overnight, and somebody stole it. I'll bet it was those Egan kids. My father was mad because the shovel got stolen. I was madder because somebody went in our clubhouse.

Today we're having a meeting of the Defense Club. I'm president. Angel didn't want to be vice-president, so my friend Neil is, and his sister Gloria is secretary and treasurer. Angel is a member of the club, but he doesn't come to every meeting.

I can see the clubhouse through the trees. The little American flag is over the door, which is the signal that a member is inside. Now I can see the eagle I drew on the door. Under the eagle Neil printed "PRIVATE, KEEP OUT."

Dukie and I jump over the moat. I knock on the door, three short knocks and two long—the secret outside knock. From inside I hear the secret inside knock—three long and two short.

"Pearl," someone inside whispers.

"Harbor." I talk very close to the door with my hand hiding my mouth.

I hear the hook latch being lifted, and Neil opens the door.

"Hi, Neil."

"Hi, Eddie."

The clubhouse floor is just dirt, but we flattened out a big cardboard box and put it down like a rug. Gloria is sitting in one corner reading a movie magazine.

"Hi, Gloria," I say.

She nods her head but doesn't look up.

Dukie is sniffing around inside the clubhouse.

"He's going to wet in here like last time," Neil reminds me.

"Come on, Duke." I let him outside, and he starts sniffing a tree.

"Where's Angel?" Neil asks, and he locks the door again.

"Playing ball," I say. "He's not coming."

I kneel down and open the secret panel Uncle Hugo made in one wall. I take out a small hammer, a notebook, a pencil, and the picture of President Roosevelt I cut out of *Life* magazine. I pull a thumbtack out of the wall and stick up the picture. Then I sit down under it, hit the hammer on the cardboard rug, and say, "The meeting will come to order."

Neil sits facing me, but Gloria is still in the corner reading.

Bang! Bang! Bang!

I hit the hammer against the wall, where it makes more noise.

"The meeting will come to order, Gloria," I say.

"Just let me finish reading about Veronica Lake," she says. "Isn't she beautiful?"

On the page Gloria shows us there's a picture of Veronica Lake wearing a shiny evening gown. Her long blond hair is hanging down over one eye. She's called "the girl with the peek-a-boo bang."

"Gloria's letting her hair grow so she can have a peek-a-boo bang," Neil tells me.

"Is there a law against that?" Gloria says. Her hair is dark brown and in two short pigtails that stick out behind her ears.

"In the first place, your hair is not blond," Neil sneers, "and in the second place, Mommy wouldn't let you have a peek-a-boo bang."

Bang! Bang! Bang! I hammer on the wall.

"This meeting of the Defense Club will now come to order." I hand Gloria the notebook and pencil. "Here, Madam Secretary."

"Thanks." She opens the notebook on top of the movie magazine in her lap.

"Roll call," I say. "Neil Maloney."

"Here."

"Gloria Maloney."

"Here."

"Angel Ferrari."

"Absent," Neil says, and Gloria marks it in the book.

36

"Eddie Ferrari. Here," I answer myself. "Will the secretary read the minutes of the last meeting?"

Gloria is turning pages in the notebook.

"The meeting was called to order," she reads. "All the members were present. The dues for the month were collected. We had eighty cents in the treasury. We talked about getting a shovel to finish the moat. Angel said he'd ask Mr. D'Andrea if we could borrow his shovel. The meeting was adjourned."

"May we have the treasurer's report?" I say.

Gloria opens the big old pocketbook she always carries. She takes out the change purse and empties it. Nickels and dimes and a folded slip of paper fall out on the cardboard rug.

"Seventy cents in cash," she reports, "and a ten-cent IOU."

That's a surprise.

"What do you mean IOU, Madam Treasurer?"

Gloria makes fun of my surprised look and says, "I didn't have the ten cents dues last month, so I wrote an IOU."

"That's 'cause you're always buying movie magazines," Neil teases.

"Shut up!" Gloria snaps.

Bang! Bang! Bang!

"Order," I say.

I read the slip of paper. "I owe the Defense Club ten cents. (signed) Gloria Maloney.

"You'd better put your dime in before the next meeting, Gloria."

"Don't worry, Mr. President," and she puts the money and the IOU back in her pocketbook.

"Any old business?" I continue the meeting. Neil raises his hand.

"Vice-President Maloney," I say.

"Mr. President, we don't know yet about Mr. D'Andrea's shovel because Angel is absent."

"That's right," I say. "Any new business?"

Neil raises his hand again.

"Vice-President Maloney."

"I make a motion that we raise the dues a nickel to fifteen cents a month."

"I second the motion," I say. "All those in favor say 'Aye.'"

"Aye," Neil and I say.

"All those opposed?" I look at Gloria.

She's reading the movie magazine again.

"Gloria!" I yell. "Aren't you taking the minutes?"

"Oh, sure." She pulls the notebook out from under the magazine.

"Madam Secretary," I say, "would you please read the motion that was just made and seconded?"

Gloria holds the notebook real close to her face.

"Gee," she mumbles, "I wrote so fast I can't read my own handwriting."

"We just said it," I say. "Can't you remember what it was?"

"Well, if you just said it, why don't *you* remember what it was?"

"We know what it was," Neil says, "but you weren't paying attention. You were too busy reading about Veronica Lake."

"She's more interesting than this dumb meeting."

Bang! Bang! Bang!

"The meeting will please come to order! We're not following parliamentary procedure."

"The hell with parliamentary procedure!" Gloria stands up.

"You cursed!" Neil says. "I'm going to tell Mommy."

"And I'm going to tell her that you and Billy Halpern wanted me to play Doctor, and you both tried to pull my dress up."

"That's a lie! You can't prove it!"

"You can't prove that you didn't!"

"I make a motion that this meeting be adjourned," I say. "Does anyone second the motion?"

Gloria takes her pocketbook and magazine and goes out the door.

"If you tell Mommy that lie," Neil yells, "I won't let you use my skates!"

"Who cares!" Gloria yells back.

Neil runs out of the clubhouse.

"Gloria! Gloria!" I hear him calling.

Dukie sticks his head inside the open doorway. When he sees me, he comes in wagging his tail.

"Meeting adjourned," I say.

I take down President Roosevelt's picture and put it and the rest of the stuff back behind the secret panel. I go out and take down the American flag, roll it up, and put it high on a ledge inside where it won't fall. The American flag must never touch the ground.

"Come on, Dukie."

I wish there was a lock on the outside of the clubhouse door. When we collect enough dues, the first thing we're going to buy is a padlock.

★ 6 ★

BB Gun

Plink!
I hit it!
I take aim again and pull the trigger.
Missed.
I take aim. This time I concentrate on holding the BB gun real steady and *squeeze* the trigger.
Plink! A hit!
I'm in the backyard having target practice. Uncle Hugo is taking basic training in Oklahoma, where he's learning to shoot all kinds of guns and throw hand grenades. I wonder if he's learning to drive a tank. Basic training takes eight weeks, just about what's left of my summer vacation. I hope it doesn't go by as fast as the last two and a half weeks. If I practice every day, my aim should be perfect by the time school starts in September.

For a target, I'm using an old tin can that had tomatoes in it. The kind my mother puts in her spaghetti sauce. It's the biggest can I could find. When it gets too easy to hit, I'll change to a smaller one. After I'm through using them, I'll give these cans to the next Scrap Drive.

"Eddie," my mother calls through the kitchen window. "What are you doing?"

"Target practice," I answer.

"Be careful. Don't shoot any BBs into the Victory garden."

"I'm being careful."

"How about doing some weeding this afternoon?" she says. "Those vegetables need room to grow."

"O.K.," I say.

The Victory garden is all the way in the other corner of the yard. My father would be mad if I hurt any of the vegetables he planted. With food scarce on account of the war, lots of people have Victory gardens. Except for the tomatoes, I can't tell the weeds from the vegetables. Anyway, pulling weeds feels even less like winning the war than collecting scrap.

"Come on, Duke, let's go on patrol."

Dunwoodie Street is paved only up to our house. The part Dukie and I are on now looks like a dried-up river bottom. The ground on each side slopes up to empty lots.

"We're on an island in the South Pacific, Duke. Our mission is to infiltrate the enemy lines. You're in the Canine Corps. All around us there's a jungle filled with snakes, malaria mosquitoes, and Jap snipers in the trees."

I pick up Dukie. Dunwoodie Street is a river full of crocodiles, and I have to step from rock to rock to get across. Crocs are snapping at my heels.

"We made it, Duke."

I put Dukie down, and he walks right back into the middle of the crocodiles and wets on a rock. We climb the slope to where the trees and bushes are thick. My BB gun is an M-1 rifle. A Jap sniper lines me up in his sights. Just as he pulls the trigger, I spot him and drop to the ground. His bullet misses, but I lie still so he'll think I'm hit. He climbs down from his tree, bayonet ready to finish me off. My finger is on the trigger, waiting for the right moment. He's walking very quietly. I hope I hear him in time. All of a sudden I feel Dukie's wet nose and tongue in my face. He wants to play. I get up and wipe my face with my sleeve.

"Here, boy." I pick up a stick and wave it in front of Dukie.

He tries to grab it in his mouth, growling his playful growl. I throw the stick into the bushes. Dukie chases it and finds it real fast. He stands with the stick in his mouth, wagging his tail and waiting for me.

"Good boy."

He drops the stick, and I throw it high into a bunch of trees. It crashes through the leaves, and Dukie is already in the bushes underneath, waiting.

He doesn't come out so fast this time. Maybe he can't find it.

"Dukie," I call.

He doesn't come. I walk over to the trees. Dukie is sitting very still looking up into a tree. When he sees me, he wags his tail and turns his head back to the tree. He stands up, turns around whining, and sits again looking up at the same tree. The stick is caught in one of the branches—not too high up, but higher than I can reach.

"I'll get it down, Duke." I put my BB gun up to my shoulder. "I'll bet I can shoot it down."

My sight is set on the stick. I hold my breath and squeeze the trigger. The BB tears through some leaves but misses the stick. I try again. This time I hit the branch the stick is caught on, but the stick doesn't budge.

I take aim, and just as I'm about to shoot, a little brown bird lands on the branch. I move my gun a few inches to the right, and instead of the stick, I've got the bird in my sight. I squeeze the trigger, and the bird gives a loud chirp and falls to the ground. Dukie runs to where the bird is flapping its wings trying to fly.

46

"No, Dukie! No!" I shoo him away.

I don't know what to do. The poor bird is suffering, and it's my fault. Hunters never leave a wounded animal to suffer, so I shoot BBs into the bird until it's dead. I feel awful.

"Get away, Dukie."

He's trying to sniff the dead bird. I don't know what he'd do if he got it in his mouth. I have to bury it. The bird looks terrible with its beak wide open. I can't pick it up with my bare hands, so I take out my handkerchief. It's a real small bird, and it feels funny even wrapped in the handkerchief.

I find a flat rock for digging a grave. Dukie keeps sticking his nose in the hole to see what I'm doing. When the grave is about twelve inches deep, I put the bird in it and push the dirt back fast. Then I cover it over with leaves. I wave a stick for Dukie and throw it. He chases it. I hope he forgets about the bird, but I can't think of anything else. I feel sick.

From its color I figure the bird was probably female. What if she was out looking for a worm to take to her babies in the nest? With no mother to feed them, those babies will starve to death, and that's my fault, too.

This is the worst thing I ever did. I hope nobody finds out. Dukie comes over with the new stick in his mouth. I kneel down and put my arm around his neck.

"You're the only one who knows, Dukie."

He squirms away and barks for me to play with him. He'll never understand the terrible thing I did. I throw the stick, and Dukie crashes through the bushes after it. I look at the BB gun in my hand and start for home to weed the Victory garden.

I leave the gun in the basement, and when I go upstairs, Dukie is in the kitchen wagging his tail and watching my mother. The chicken soup she's making smells good. She puts in rice and celery, and meatballs as small as marbles.

"O.K., here," she says and gives Dukie a piece of chicken skin.

You're never supposed to give dogs chicken bones because they choke on them. I think about the bird and wonder if her hungry babies are waiting for their dinner.

The phone rings.

"Eddie," my mother says, "will you get that? And tell whoever it is that I'll call them back."

"Hello," I say into the phone.

"Is this Eddie Ferrari?" a strange, low, shaky voice says.

"Yes. Who's this?"

There isn't any answer right away, and then the voice says, "Beware."

"Who *is* this?"

Click.

"Hello. Hello!"

They've hung up. I try to think whose voice that could have been. It sounded like some kid talking deep and shaking the way you do when you're trying not to laugh, and I think I heard giggling in the background.

"Who was it?" my mother says.

"I don't know. Wrong number."

I walk into the living room. Maybe it was Neil horsing around, but he would have called right back to see if I was fooled. I know. I'll bet it was those Egans. What if they saw me shoot the bird? I'll never hear the end of it, and everybody will find out. I wish I could undo what I did.

Meatless Tuesday

"Can you eat another half a sandwich each?" my mother asks.

"I can," Angel says. He has a white mustache from drinking his milk.

"I can, too," I say.

"Angel, wipe your mouth," my mother says. "Not on your hand. Where's your napkin?"

"On the floor," I say.

It's hard to keep a paper napkin on your lap. I tuck mine under my belt.

Angel picks up his napkin and waves it in the air.

"This is a Jap Zero. *Rrrrrrrr!*" He makes the sound of an airplane. "It's flying low on a strafing mission." He picks up his fork. "John Wayne is manning a machine gun on the ground. *A-a-a-a-a-a-a-a!*" Angel sticks the fork through the napkin and makes a big rip. "A direct hit!"

My mother gives Angel a dirty look. She doesn't like it when we play War. Angel holds the napkin as high as he can and lets it go. As it flutters to the floor, he makes the sound of a plane in a tailspin. Then he goes, *"POUGGGH!"* for the crash.

"Are you finished?" My mother sounds annoyed. "Will I be glad when school starts."

"Oh, Ma," I say, "we still have seven weeks of vacation."

"Here, eat." My mother gives each of us half an egg salad sandwich. "And this is a napkin." She tucks a new one under Angel's chin. "If you're going to act like a baby, you should wear a bib like a baby."

Angel is smiling. His dimples show.

I lean over my plate to bite my sandwich because some egg salad always leaks out of the bottom. Today is Meatless Tuesday. Meat is scarce because of the war, so President Roosevelt asked all Americans not to eat meat one day a week. He picked Tuesday.

After lunch Angel and I head for the clubhouse. Yesterday afternoon I saw the Egan kids coming out of our clubhouse, but they didn't see me. I was so surprised I forgot all about yelling, "Heil, Egan!" Today I called an emergency meeting of the Defense Club.

"What are you going to do with that picture?" Angel asks.

"Hang it in the clubhouse," I say.

I cut this poster out of *Life* magazine. It shows a finger pressed against a pair of lips and a ship with lots of black smoke coming out of it sinking in the ocean. In big letters it says, "ZIP YOUR LIP OR SINK A SHIP." People shouldn't talk about where servicemen they know are going or when they are leaving because spies could be anywhere listening.

We pass Jim the Hermit's shack.

"I wonder what it's like to be a hermit?" I say.

"Lonely," Angel says. "But I'll bet it's fun to have kerosene lamps and a wood stove like in a Western."

"How do you know he has those things?"

"One day Freddy and I looked in his window."

"Weren't you scared he'd see you?"

"We saw Jim going someplace. That's when we snuck a look."

"What else was in there?"

"There were newspapers stuck up like wallpaper and old pieces of rug on the floor. He has a small bed, and there's an old, beat-up table, a couple of orange crates, magazines, two kerosene lamps, the stove. . . . That's all I remember."

"Was there an aerial on the roof?"

"I didn't notice. Freddy wanted to go inside,

but there was a big padlock on the door, and the window was locked from the inside."

"I think he's a saboteur or a spy," I tell my brother.

"You're crazy." Angel laughs.

"Remember the blackout a few weeks ago?" I ask.

"Yes."

"Well, I was looking out the upstairs bathroom window. Everything was blacked out, and I saw a light, blinking like a signal, coming from Jim's shack."

"Freddy says Jim gets drunk a lot. Maybe he just forgot to close his blackout curtains."

"But the light was blinking," I say. "Somebody had to be doing that."

"I don't know." Angel wrinkles his nose. "He doesn't look like a spy to me."

"That's what I mean. He's somebody nobody would suspect."

We're heading toward the tree where the bird is buried.

"Let's go this way." I hope I don't sound guilty. "It's easier."

We turned onto the narrow footpath that leads to the clubhouse. I almost tell Angel about the bird. I'd like him to know what a good shot I am, but I feel so bad that I killed it, I'll never tell anyone. And I don't know if I should say

anything about the mysterious phone call. What if it wasn't the Egans but somebody else who saw me? I decide not to mention it.

The American flag isn't up outside the clubhouse, so I guess nobody's there, unless those Egans are. I signal Angel to be quiet, and we sneak up to the door. I listen. If anybody is inside, they're not making a sound. With my hand on the door handle, I look at Angel. He nods his head, and I push open the door. The clubhouse is empty.

"Lock the door," I say when we're inside. "Wait a minute. The flag."

Angel puts the American flag up outside, then comes back in and latches the door. I take the things out of the secret panel and put up President Roosevelt's picture and the "ZIP YOUR LIP" poster.

"I hear somebody coming," Angel says.

The only window in the clubhouse is in back. It's really just a slit Uncle Hugo made for ventilation. You can't see much out of it. Whoever is coming up to the door isn't trying to be quiet. Three short knocks and two long. Angel knocks back three long and two short.

"Pearl," he says.

I recognize Neil's voice when he whispers, "Harbor."

Angel opens the door.

"Hi," Angel and I say.

"Hi." Neil comes in. "What's the emergency?"

"The Egan kids are using the clubhouse," I say.

"What are we going to do?" Neil asks.

"That's what we have to decide at this meeting," Angel tells him.

"We have to get a padlock," I say. "If we collect next month's dues in advance, I think we'll have enough money to buy one. Where's Gloria?"

"She's coming," Neil says. "She was washing her hair."

"Didn't she know this was an emergency?" I say.

"I told her. Then as soon as my mother went to the store, Gloria decided to wash her hair."

"We shouldn't have made her treasurer," I say.

"I think we ought to make up a new password." Angel changes the subject. "Pearl Harbor is too easy to figure out."

"That's right," Neil says.

Pearl Harbor was my idea, but I guess it is too easy.

"O.K.," I agree, "let's think of a new one."

"Wait a second," Neil says, "we're not following parliamentary procedure."

"I know, Neil, but I can't call the meeting to

57

order until Gloria gets here. Was she almost finished washing her hair?"

"I don't know. She was in the bathroom with the door locked."

"While we're waiting," I say, "let's think up a bunch of new passwords. Then in the meeting we'll vote for one. I'll make a list."

I take the notebook Gloria writes the minutes in and turn to the last page. There are names written all over it in every direction. First "Gloria Maloney" is written about ten times. Then, "Sincerely yours, Veronica Lake," then, "Veronica Maloney" real big with a fancy *V* and the tail of the *y* all swirly, and "For all my fans, Gloria Lake." The rest of the page is filled with "Gloria Lake." I turn to the next to the last page.

"How about United States for a password?" Neil begins.

"Too easy," Angel says, but I write it down anyway.

"How about Meatless Tuesday?" I say and write it down.

"That's silly." Neil makes a face.

"It's better than United States." I make a face back and stick out my tongue.

"I know," Angel says, "Zip Your Lip."

"Too many words," Neil criticizes.

We're all thinking.

I get an idea. "Instead of Zip Your Lip, how about Zipped Lips?"

"That's not bad," Neil says, and I write it on the list.

"*Shhh!*" Angel says. "Somebody's coming."

We all listen. "I don't hear anything," I say.

"How about . . ." Neil starts to say.

Bang!

There's a knock at the door. Not exactly a knock but more as if somebody threw something.

We wait for the secret outside knock, but everything is quiet. I unlatch the door and open it slowly. Nobody's there, but lying on the ground is a rock with a piece of paper attached by a rubber band.

"Who is it?" Angel sticks his head out.

"Somebody threw a rock," I say, "with a note."

I pick up the rock, and the rubber band breaks when I take off the paper. I put the rubber band in my pocket for the next Scrap Drive.

"Look!" I say to Angel.

The piece of paper has "BEWARE" printed on it, with a skull and crossbones drawn underneath.

"Just like the phone call," I blurt out.

"What phone call?" Angel asks.

"I'll tell you later."

"What is it?" Neil comes outside.

We look around trying to see who threw the rock. Anybody could be hiding in the bushes or up a tree. I wish Dukie was here. He'd sniff them out.

⋆ 8 ⋆

Sneak Attack

"Charge!" Richie Egan shouts.

He, Mikey, and Peggy come crashing out of the bushes. They're waving sticks and whooping like Indians.

"Inside, quick!" I say, pushing Neil and Angel inside the clubhouse and slamming the door behind us. I'm so excited I can't get the hook in the latch, but I do just as one of the Egans bangs a stick against the door. The clubhouse is surrounded. All the walls are being beaten with sticks, and the whooping and hollering is ferocious.

"I've got my water pistol," Neil says. He goes to the slit of a window and waits for one of the Egan kids to pass.

"Hey!" somebody outside yells.

"I squirted Mikey in the head," Neil says, smiling.

"Let me," Angel says, and Neil hands him the water pistol.

The whooping stops, and we hear scraping sounds outside one wall. Then a thud on the roof.

The whooping and beating start again, and now somebody's jumping up and down on the roof, too.

"I got Richie right in the face." Angel smiles.

"Give me a turn," I say.

"Here," Angel says.

I see Mikey run past the slit, but just a short squirt comes out of the water pistol and misses him. Then Richie is coming right toward the slit. I wait till he's real close and pull the trigger, but nothing happens. The water pistol is empty. I turn away just as Richie throws a handful of dirt. It hits the back of my head.

That must be Peggy on the roof. It sounds as if she's going to stomp right through it.

"We can't stay in here," Angel says.

"Right," I say. "Get ready to counterattack. When I open the door, we'll rush them. Angel, you take Mikey. Neil, don't let Peggy off the roof. I'll take Richie." My hand is on the hook. "Remember to whoop and yell. Ready? Charge!"

I unhook the latch and pull. The door doesn't budge, and Neil and Angel bump into me.

"What's the matter?" Angel says.

"I don't know," I say.

Angel pulls the door.

"They must be holding it from outside," Neil guesses.

"Let's all pull." Angel grabs the door.

Neil puts his arms around Angel's waist, and I put mine around Neil's.

"O.K., now!" Angel shouts.

The door bends a little, but that's all.

The beating stops. Only the stomping on the roof keeps up.

"Get off the roof," Richie says.

We hear Peggy climb down. The Egan kids are laughing and whispering.

"You are our prisoners!" Richie yells through the slit. "Do you surrender?"

"Never!" I yell back. "I dare you to come in and get us."

I wish the water pistol was loaded.

Richie laughs and says, "This is your last chance to surrender."

Angel and Neil and I look at each other.

"We're trapped." Neil sounds worried.

"Shut up," I say.

"Give up?" Richie calls.

I get real close to the slit and yell, "No! Never!"

"O.K." Richie's talking like a big wheel. "Stay right there till you starve."

More whispering and laughing.

> *Eddie Spaghetti—*
> *Put him in a pot.*
> *Turn on the fire*
> *And watch him get hot.*

"Good-bye," Richie says. "We'll be back for your bones." His voice sounds as if he's walking away.

"Let us out! Let us out!" Neil yells and pulls on the door. He's scared.

"Good night!" Richie sounds real far away. "Sleep tight."

It seems like a long time since we heard anything from outside. I thought Richie was just trying to scare us, but now I think they really left us locked in.

"If we all yell 'Help!' together, somebody has to hear us." Neil's chin is trembling.

"And suppose they're just hiding out in the bushes?" I say. "They'd love to hear that."

"We have the hammer," Angel reminds me. "Let's break through one of the walls."

I hate to damage the clubhouse, but there's no other way out.

"I'll take some nails out to loosen the wall," I say.

With the back of the hammer, I pry out a long nail.

"Hurry," Neil whispers.

"Don't be such a fraidycat," Angel says.

I have another nail halfway out when there are three short and two long knocks on the door.

"Gloria!" Neil yells. "We're locked in! Help us!"

I smell smoke and see it coming in through a crack in the door.

"It's them again!" Neil wails. "They're setting us on fire!"

"Who's there?" Angel yells. "Come on Richie, this isn't funny."

More smoke. Then a scraping sound, and the door swings open. Neil runs out.

"Gloria!" I hear him say. "You're smoking. Oh, Gloria, what did you do to your hair?"

Angel and I walk out of the clubhouse. Gloria is standing there with her big old pocketbook hanging from her shoulder. The strap broke, so she tied on a long piece of clothesline. She's puffing on a cigarette, and her hair is blond, and instead of pigtails she has a very short peek-a-boo bang. She doesn't look much like Veronica Lake.

"How did you make your hair blond?" I ask.

"Some special stuff that movie stars use. It was advertised in a movie magazine, and I sent away for some."

"Does Mommy know?" Neil says.

"Of course." Gloria blows smoke in his face. "She said I look beautiful."

"Liar," Neil coughs.

"How did you get locked in?" she asks.

"Those Egan kids snuck up on us," Neil says.

"What was holding the door closed?" Angel asks.

"That." Gloria points to a wide, wooden plank. "It was wedged through the handle and across the door like a bolt."

"Where's the flag?" Angel says. "It's not up over the door."

"Here." I pick it up out of the dirt. "They even disgraced the American flag."

"They could attack again," Neil says, "when we're all inside having a meeting."

"We'll have to take turns standing guard," Angel says.

"And lock the clubhouse when we're not here," I add. "If we all pay July's dues in advance, that will be forty cents plus the eighty cents in the treasury—enough for a good padlock."

"Gloria," Neil says, "did you put in the ten cents you owe?"

"Not yet," she says.

"So there's only seventy cents in the treasury," I say. "Just hand it over, Gloria."

She throws away the cigarette and starts looking through her pocketbook.

"I can't seem to find my change purse."

"I'll find it," Neil says and grabs her pocketbook.

Gloria screams and tries to grab it back.

"The change purse is right here," Neil says, "and it's empty."

We all look at Gloria.

"Where's the money?" Angel wants to know.

"Give me my pocketbook." Neil gives it to her. "I borrowed it," Gloria confesses. "I didn't have enough to buy a money order for the hair bleach." She takes out a mirror and looks in it. "I'll put a nickel from my allowance in every week till I pay it back."

"That'll take months," I say. "We need a lock immediately. All those who want a new treasurer raise your hand."

Angel, Neil and I raise our hands.

"Ha, ha," Neil laughs.

"What happened to your stupid parliamentary procedure?" Gloria says, really snippy.

"Don't worry." I give her a dirty look. "We'll have a meeting to choose candidates, and then we'll have an election."

Gloria puts the mirror back in her pocketbook and takes out a liverwurst sandwich wrapped in wax paper.

"Don't you know today's Meatless Tuesday?" I say. "You're unpatriotic."

Gloria takes a big bite out of the sandwich and walks away.

★ 9 ★
Spying

I feel worse today than the day after Pearl Harbor. The Egan kids' sneak attack yesterday was a big defeat for the Defense Club. We have to secure our clubhouse and plan a counterattack. That's if there still is a Defense Club. Angel and Neil don't want to be in it if Gloria is.

Mrs. Maloney was furious when she saw Gloria's hair. She said, "Nice girls don't bleach their hair," and gave Gloria a real short boy's haircut. Neil says his sister wears a kerchief on her head all the time and hardly ever goes outside. I don't feel sorry for her.

It's been raining real hard, and now Dunwoodie Street really does look like a river full of crocodiles. Angel is over at Freddy's, and my mother had to go to the drugstore, so I'm home alone. If my mother's not back by a quarter to one, I have to listen to *Our Gal Sunday*, one of her soap operas, and tell her what happens.

Dukie is out, too, and now he's scratching on the back door. He must be soaked. I get his towel off its hook and go to let him in. He dashes inside and stops to shake the rain off.

"Dukie, come here."

I have to dry him before he goes into the living room, but out of the corner of my eye I see something moving outside. It's Jim the Hermit, and he's practically in our backyard! I quickly lock the back door and run to the kitchen window. Jim's just passing by, walking close to our yard to keep out of the tall, wet grass in the empty lot. He's wearing a coat way too big for him (like me in my father's clothes), and the black umbrella over his head is broken and torn. I go to the living room. I can see better from those windows. Oh, no! Dukie is in here shaking water on the wallpaper.

"Come here, Duke,"

I throw his towel over him and rub. He thinks I'm playing.

"Let go!"

He's got one corner of the towel in his mouth. We're having a tug-of-war.

"Stay off the sofa," I say, and drop my end of the towel. I look outside just in time to see Jim the Hermit walk out of sight.

I dry Dukie's paws the best I can. He keeps chewing the towel. I check the time: twenty-five after twelve. Even if Jim is just going to get something to eat, he should be gone at least half an hour. This would be a good time to take a look in his shack. It's scary to think of, but this is wartime. I have to be brave.

I put on my raincoat, rainhat, and galoshes. I wish I could take Dukie with me, but the orange tiger might be around. I wonder if that cat attacks like a watchdog. *I have to be brave.*

There aren't any kids out playing in the empty lots. Rain is good camouflage for a secret mission. I walk through the wet grass toward the shack. Every once in a while I look over my shoulder to make sure Jim isn't coming back. The clump of trees is right in front of me, and I can see part of the tin roof all shiny from the rain. The air is hot and humid, but I feel a chill. Maybe I should do this some other time. *Be brave.*

I'm standing right next to the shack now. I never thought I'd ever be this close. The rain on the tin roof is making a racket, but there isn't any aerial up there.

I look in the window. It's just the way Angel said it was. Some of the newspapers on the wall are funny pages. I wonder if my mother would let me wallpaper my room with my favorite comic strips.

I don't see the orange tiger anywhere. Maybe it's out chasing field mice. There's another win-

dow on the other side of the shack, so I walk around to look in it. It's open a crack. I push, and it swings open all the way. I unbutton my raincoat so I can get my leg up high enough to climb inside.

I'm standing in the middle of Jim the Hermit's shack! When I tell Neil, he'll never believe me. I'll bet Richie Egan wouldn't be brave enough to do it. I'd better hurry and search the place. I look under the rugs for a trapdoor. Nothing. On the table there's a cigar box full of string, nails, and screws. I look along the walls for a secret panel. I find a great *Dick Tracy* strip in color but no secret hiding place. The rain on the roof makes an even bigger racket inside. Jim's bed is very neatly made up. I look under it. There's something! A big, old chest like the kind pirates bury treasure in.

I can't pull the chest out far enough to open it, so I crawl behind it to push, and I'm face to face with Jim's big old tiger cat. I close my eyes tight, cover them with my hands, and start crawling backward on my elbows and knees. Any second I expect to feel claws on my face. The cat isn't making a sound. I take a chance and peek through my fingers. The cat's gone.

I crawl out from under the bed fast. I'm still on my knees when I see the black umbrella pass the window. I dive back under the bed just as Jim the Hermit comes in the door. I feel the floorboards shake. All of a sudden I hear a loud groan, the floorboards shake again, and then the only sound is the rain on the roof.

★ 10 ★

The Doughboy

I don't know what to do. Jim is probably holding a machine gun waiting for me to come out. If I had a white handkerchief, I'd wave it.

"I surrender," I say, and crawl out.

While I'm still on my knees, I put my hands up. The shack is empty. I jump to my feet and run for the door.

"*Aaah!*" I gasp.

Jim the Hermit is outside blocking my way. He's holding a shovel up like a club.

"Inside before I crack your skull!" Jim's voice is gravelly. It's the first time I've ever heard it. His face is purple, and there's a raindrop hanging on the end of his nose.

I've never been so scared in my life. Nobody would hear me if I yelled for help. I back into the shack. If I wasn't wearing my raincoat and galoshes, I might be fast enough to get out through the window.

"What were you looking for? What do you want?" Jim asks. His eyes look more scared than angry.

"Nothing," I say.

"I could have you arrested," Jim says. "You hooligan!"

I'm up against the back wall. The shovel is shaking in Jim's hand, and any second I expect it to come crashing down on my head. I've got to do something fast. *Be brave.*

"That's my shovel," I say. "You stole it from our clubhouse."

"I never did. I found it in the woods."

"You can tell that to the police."

"Can you prove it's your shovel?"

"My father painted our name on it. There on the handle."

Jim lowers the shovel.

"Ferrari?" he says. "Is that your name?"

"Yes," I say and get ready to make a run for it.

"Is that why you broke in? Looking for the shovel?"

"Yes," I lie.

"I only borrowed it. I would have put it back. Why don't you kids leave me alone?" Jim's voice sounds funny, as if he's going to cry. "Here, take it."

Jim leans the shovel against the table and goes over to sit on the bed. He looks small in that big coat.

"I'm sorry I broke in," I say.

"Doesn't matter. Where's my cat? You didn't hurt him?"

"No, he scared me."

"More likely the other way around. He's shy of strangers. *Psss! Psss! Psss!* Here, Sunny. It's all right. Don't be scared."

The rain sounds louder than ever. I take the shovel and walk to the door. It must be about one o'clock (I missed *Our Gal Sunday*), but it's almost dark as night outside. Jim takes something wrapped in waxed paper out of his coat pocket.

"Come on, Sunny boy."

He opens the waxed paper and puts it on the floor. Sunny's head pops out of a cardboard box in the corner. He jumps out, walks head down and tail up over to the paper, and starts eating what's inside. I feel dumb standing there. I wish I'd never come.

"Chicken gizzard," Jim says. "He loves it."

The roof is leaking over the table. Jim puts a tin can on the table to catch the drops.

"Raining cats and dogs," he says. "You'd better wait till it lets up a mite. I hate rain. Turns everything to mud."

I can't think of anything to say. All I'm thinking is that I want to leave, but the rain is like a solid wall.

"We could be inside Niagara Falls." Jim laughs. Some of his teeth are missing. "That's a good one. Ever been to Niagara Falls?"

"No."

"Me neither. Been across the Atlantic Ocean, though."

"Did you go on the *Queen Mary*?"

Jim laughs again. "Weren't no *Queen Mary* in 1917. No, sir, was a crowded troop ship transporting doughboys over to France."

"Doughboys?"

"That's what they called American infantrymen in World War I."

"You were in World War I?" I say.

"Yes indeed. Over in those muddy trenches fighting. I'll show you."

Jim pulls the chest all the way out from under the bed. The lid makes a scraping sound when he opens it. I walk over to look.

"Here's my uniform." Jim takes out a hat with a wide brim, and a neatly folded jacket and pants. Everything's khaki colored.

He puts on the hat and takes off his raincoat. The T-shirt he has on is also too big for him and has a big hole in it. He puts on the khaki jacket. It buttons all the way up to his neck.

"Still fits," he says. "Private First Class Lockhart reporting." He salutes. "Want to try it on?" And he hands me the hat.

"O.K.," I say.

"No mirror," Jim says, "but I'll light the lamp, and maybe you can see your reflection in the windowpane, being it's so dark out."

He holds the lighted lamp near me, and I see myself in the window. I look silly with the hat down over my ears.

"Give it here," Jim says. "Too big."

He stuffs rolled-up newspaper inside the headband. "Try it now."

I look at myself again. It fits perfectly.

"Look here." Jim unbuttons the left breast pocket of the Army jacket. "My sharpshooter's medal. Let me pin it on you."

"No, thanks." I think of the bird. "You won it. Pin it on yourself."

"Yes, sir, I was a real good shot." He pins the medal over the pocket he took it out of.

"Did you have to shoot anybody?" I ask.

"Sure did."

"Were they killed?"

"They went down. Guess I killed some."

"Did it make you feel bad?"

"In a war," Jim says, "you got to kill the enemy before he kills you. You don't have time to think about it."

Jim sits on the bed, reaches into the chest, and takes out a fancy box with "Bonbon" written on it.

81

"That's French for *candy*," he says. But instead of candy the box is full of photographs and letters. "That's me in France."

He shows me a picture of a thin young soldier sitting in a horse and buggy. There's a pretty girl sitting next to him with her head resting on his shoulder. The soldier and the girl are smiling straight at me. I look at Jim and back at the picture. It's hard to believe that he's that young soldier.

"Is she your girlfriend?" I ask.

"Was." He takes the picture and looks at it. "Lived in a nice little house in a nice little town. Her father was the *forgeron*. That means blacksmith. I guess I wanted to marry her, so after the armistice I came back to America, worked, and saved my money. These are her letters, all written in French."

"Do you understand French?" I say.

"I picked up a couple of words, but to read the letters I got me this here dictionary, translates French into English. She had the schoolmaster in her town translate my letters. After about a year came this letter written in English." He holds it up. "From her father, but he didn't write it. Dictated it to the schoolmaster. Said his daughter couldn't wait for me no longer. She was married. Can you guess to who?"

82

"The schoolmaster?"

"You guessed it." Jim sits there looking at the picture. The rain must have stopped because it's real quiet now. "But that's all water under the bridge." He puts the picture and letter back in the candy box. "Just look at that cat." Sunny is curled up inside the chest. "Come on, Mr. Curiosity," and Jim gently lifts Sunny out and puts him on the bed.

"I have to go," I say, and give Jim his hat. "Thanks."

"My name's Jim," Jim the Hermit says. "What's yours?"

"Eddie."

"Pleased to meet you." We shake hands.

"How come you live in this shack?" I ask.

"Ten years ago was hard times in this country. You're too young to remember. Lots of people living in shanties like this one. But that's another story. Come and see me again sometime, but don't sneak in the window. You scared me half to death."

"I'm sorry," I say.

"I'm sorry, too," Jim says, "about borrowing the shovel. That makes us even."

I take the shovel and walk to the door.

" 'Bye," I say.

"So long."

The sky is still dark, but it isn't raining anymore except when the wind blows through the trees and shakes the rain off the leaves. I guess I was wrong about Jim being a spy, but he could be a traitor. I stop and look back toward the shack, and there's the blinking light just like the night of the blackout! But now I see what's making it. When the wind blows, the bushes around Jim's shack sway back and forth across the window. It was windy that night, and Jim must not have turned his light off right away.

"Where were you?" my mother says.

"Out," I say.

"I figured that out for myself. Where?"

"I went over to the clubhouse."

"In all that rain? I had to wait in the drugstore until it stopped. What was so important?"

"I just wanted to make sure nothing was stolen."

"All of a sudden, in the middle of a rainstorm?" my mother says. "Is that our missing shovel?"

"Yes."

"Where did you find it?"

"In one of the empty lots." I don't think my mother would like it if I told her I was in Jim the Hermit's shack. And if she knew I put on his hat, she'd make me wash my hair.

"I give up." She looks at me suspiciously. "Out in the pouring rain and you just happen to find a shovel that nobody has seen for weeks. You're a regular Sherlock Holmes. Did you listen to *Our Gal Sunday*?"

"I forgot," I say.

My mother gives me one of her looks that means, "Why can't you be more dependable?" She says, "Take off those galoshes before you track up the whole house, and put that shovel in the garage."

★ 11 ★

Ambush

"Thirty minutes to zero hour," I tell Angel and Neil. "Let's go over it one more time."

We're down in the playroom having a final briefing before launching the Defense Club's counterattack against the Egans. Zero hour is fifteen hundred hours, which is military time for three o'clock in the afternoon. We've been planning our strategy every day since last week's sneak attack, and the map I drew, marked TOP SECRET, is spread out on the card table.

"I'm the black circle," says Neil, pointing, "up in this tree."

"Check," I say. "Don't lean on the table, Neil. It'll collapse. Angel, you're the . . ."

"I know," Angel interrupts, "the white circle in *this* tree."

"And I'm the triangle in this clump of bushes," I say, "where I can cover the Egans' retreat."

We're going to ambush them on the narrow footpath that leads to the clubhouse.

"The *X*'s mark the booby traps." I feel like a

general. "Remember where they are so you don't step in one by mistake."

We dug six small holes in strategic spots along the footpath and covered them over with thin twigs and leaves to look like solid ground. The holes are just deep enough to trip anybody who steps in them.

"One person might be lucky and miss the traps," I say, "but with the three Egans walking close together, at least one is bound to fall. That's when you two start bombarding them with mud grenades."

Mud grenades are something like snowballs made out of wet dirt and left overnight to dry. They don't hurt when they hit you. They just make you dirty.

"They'll probably be armed with sticks like last time," says Neil.

"But we'll be up in trees where they can't reach us," says Angel.

"What happens when we run out of mud grenades?" Neil asks.

"If you aim carefully and score enough direct hits," I tell him, "they'll be retreating by then."

"That's when we climb down," Angel says, "and pick up the sticks we hid and chase them."

"And we'll be whooping and hollering," says Neil.

"Check." I can't help smiling. "When they pass my position, I'll hit them with more grenades. Remember, Peggy's the smallest, so go easy. Direct the attack at Richie and Mikey, and let's try to take one of them prisoner."

"I've got the rope." Angel holds up a long piece of clothesline.

"Instead of running back along the footpath," Neil says, "what if they run into the clubhouse for protection?"

"That would be great!" I laugh. "We'll do what they did to us and have three prisoners." I look at my watch. "Fourteen hundred hours and forty-five minutes, time to man your battle stations. Good luck."

Angel and Neil each take a shopping bag full of mud grenades and go out through the garage. Now comes the most important part of our plan—getting the Egans to the battle zone. And I have to do it. I know they're in their backyard, because Angel went to reconnoiter just before the briefing.

I go upstairs to the telephone, pick up the receiver, and put a handkerchief over the mouthpiece. I dial the Egans' number. It's ringing. My stomach feels as if I swallowed a Mexican jumping bean.

"Hello," I hear either Richie or Mikey say.

"Is this Richie Egan?" I talk slow and make my voice as low as I can.

"Yes," Richie says.

"You are a jerk," I say, low and slow. "Your brother is a moron, and your sister picks her nose and eats it."

"Hey! Who is this?" Richie sounds mad.

"I dare the three of you to come to the Defense Clubhouse at three o'clock, but cowards never take a dare."

"Mikey, Peggy," Richie calls, "I think it's Eddie Spaghetti, and he's giving us a dare."

I hear other voices, but I can't make out what they're saying.

"What do you want, Eddie Spaghetti?" Peggy says into the phone.

"This is the voice of doom," I say lower than ever. "Beware," and I make my voice fade away like a ghost's.

> Eddie Spaghetti—
> Put him in . . .

I hang up before they finish.

I grab my shopping bag of grenades and run out the door. First I look toward their house—they aren't coming yet. Then I run as fast as I can across Dunwoodie Street and through the empty lots. No time to check Angel and Neil. I crawl into my clump of bushes. As long as I don't move, nobody will ever see me in here.

Fifteen hundred hours on the dot. I usually don't wear my wristwatch when I'm playing, but this isn't play, it's combat. The Egans must be on their way by now. I stand up for a second, but I don't see them. Maybe they didn't take my phone call seriously.

Fifteen hundred hours and five minutes. A little green inchworm is inching along a leaf right in front of my nose. That's about how fast the Egans must be walking, if they're coming. I crawl out of my hiding place and through the tall grass to where I can see more of Dunwoodie Street. No Egans or anybody else.

There is another route to the clubhouse, but I can't believe they would take it. You have to walk blocks out of the way, climb a steep embankment, where you keep sliding backward in soft dirt, and then break through thick patches of brambles and burrs with poison ivy all around. Even if they did get through that way, Angel and Neil would be bombarding them by now. It's twenty after three. They're not coming. I leave my shopping bag hidden in the bushes and walk toward the clubhouse. I watch out for the booby traps.

"Where are they?" Angel calls down from his tree.

"How should I know?" I shrug my shoulders.

"Did you dare them?" Neil calls.

"Of course," I answer.

"Maybe they're waiting to catch us off guard," Angel says.

"They also might have come the long way around," I say, "and snuck into the clubhouse." I signal Angel to stay where he is and Neil to climb down.

"Be quiet and cautious, Neil, in case they're hiding nearby," I whisper. "Sneak up and check

the clubhouse, and have your stick ready to use as a bolt. If nobody's there, climb that big tree where we play Tarzan and watch for them the long way."

I walk back and crawl into my position. I hope they're just waiting to catch us off guard like Angel said. All of a sudden I hear whooping and hollering from the clubhouse. I grab my shopping bag and start running along the footpath.

"Help!" It sounds like Neil.

Like a dope I step in the first booby trap and fall flat on my stomach with the shopping bag under me. My grenades are all smashed into dust.

"The Egans got Neil!" Angel says when I get to his tree.

A mud grenade whizzes by my head and explodes against the tree.

"And his ammo, too," I say.

"They were hiding behind the clubhouse," Angel says, "and ambushed him."

I should have figured on the long way when I planned my strategy. I'd make some general.

Richie, Mikey, and Peggy are lobbing mud grenades at us, but we're pretty well protected by trees and bushes. Angel is in a better position to fire on them, and he's made some direct hits. He looks down at me and says, "Why aren't you firing? Where's your ammo?"

"I'll tell you later," I reply.

"Help!" I hear Neil yell.

"Where is he?" I ask Angel.

"A prisoner in the clubhouse. They used his own stick for a bolt."

"It's all my fault. We have to rescue him, Angel."

"O.K., how? I only have three grenades left."

If we had more ammo, Angel could keep their attention while I circled around behind the clubhouse and let Neil out. Then we'd have the Egans sandwiched between Neil and me behind and Angel in front.

"The only thing to do," I decide, "is rush them."

"Cease fire!" Richie yells. "Cease fire!"

Angel and I look at each other.

"What are they up to now?" he says.

"Come on down," I say.

We move closer to the clubhouse. I have one of Angel's grenades in my hand just in case.

"Truce," Richie calls when he sees me and Angel.

"Not too close," I whisper to Angel. "This may be a trick."

"See, I'm unarmed." Richie shows the palms of his hands, but something might be in his pocket.

Mikey and Peggy are standing close to the club-house. She's holding Neil's shopping bag, and it looks empty. All three Egans have smudges on them where Angel's mud grenades hit them.

"What do you want?" I ask.

"Eddie!" Neil yells. "I'm locked in the club-house!"

"Quiet in there," Mikey growls.

"Or we'll give you thirty lashes," Peggy adds, and they start giggling.

"Meet me halfway, Eddie Spaghetti," Richie says. "Unarmed." And he starts walking toward me.

"Keep an eye on Mikey and Peggy." I give Angel the grenade and go to meet Richie.

"We're ready to release our prisoner," Richie brags. "Do you want him back?"

"Of course."

"O.K., but there's one condition."

That's what I was afraid of. But you should act nonchalant in front of the enemy. Cool as a cucumber I say, "Only one?" and put my hands in my pockets.

Richie flinches and almost steps back, but he's acting nonchalant, too.

"You didn't fool us on the telephone. 'The voice of doom,' ha-ha."

"I figured you'd know it was me," and I lean forward a little.

"Well, we're here just like you dared us. Can you take a dare, Eddie Spaghetti? A double dare?"

"Easy as falling off a log," I say, but there's a jumping bean in my stomach.

"All you have to do"—Richie is talking real smart-alecky—"is go up to Jim the Hermit's shack and knock on the door, and when he answers, say, 'Hi, Jim, I'm Eddie Spaghetti.' I double dare you."

★ 12 ★

The Double Dare

I almost laugh right in Richie's face. Now I don't have to *act* nonchalant. I *am* nonchalant.

"O.K." I try to sound real serious. "Anything to save a member of the Defense Club."

I walk back to where Angel's waiting.

"What do they want?" he asks.

"I have to go to Jim the Hermit's shack and say to him, 'Hi, Jim, I'm Eddie Spaghetti.' "

"Are you going to?"

"He double dared me."

The Egans are huddled in front of the clubhouse when Angel and I walk up.

"Here they are." Mikey nudges his brother and sister.

"Are you scared, Eddie Spaghetti?" Peggy asks.

"No."

"Just do the voice of doom." Mikey giggles.

"Angel can't go with you," Richie says. "He stays here."

"O.K.," I agree.

"Ready?" Richie looks me in the eye.

"Ready," and he and I start walking. "Neil!"

I yell back. "Don't worry, you'll be out in no time."

"What's going on?" Neil yells.

Angel walks over to the clubhouse and talks to him through the door.

"Let me go first," I warn Richie when we get to the footpath. "Step only where I step."

"Why?"

"Booby traps."

I'd like to see him fall just once, but it wouldn't be fair while the cease-fire is on. We cross the unpaved part of Dunwoodie Street and climb the slope toward Jim's shack. I'm still leading the way.

"You coming to the door with me?" I ask.

"No, but I'll be near enough to make sure you do it."

"Scared?" I smile.

"No, but you are." Richie looks at me funny. I'll bet he's wondering why I don't look scared.

"Don't make so much noise," Richie whispers when the shack is in sight.

"What have I got to lose? This is your idea."

"Well, I don't want him coming out and chasing us before you have a chance to knock on the door."

"Why? Afraid you'll be the one he catches?"

"Shut up."

About fifteen feet from the shack, Richie touches my shoulder and stops.

"You know what to say?" he whispers.

I nod my head. The only part about this double dare I don't like is having to say, "I'm Eddie Spaghetti." Maybe I'll just leave out the "Spaghetti."

"What if he isn't home?" I say.

"We'll come back later. I'm going behind that tree."

Richie stoops over and runs to a tree to the left of the door. He'll be able to watch me but won't be seen by Jim. I walk up to the shack and stand in front of the door. I look over at Richie. He makes a knocking motion with his fist. I knock.

There's not a sound from inside, and the windows are closed tight. I hope Jim is home. I knock again. I hear a loud thump, and then the worst curse words you can imagine. A few seconds later the door opens very slowly.

"Hi, Jim, I'm Eddie . . . Spaghetti." I say "Spaghetti" real soft.

"Eddie who? What do you want? Go away." Jim's voice sounds as if he was asleep.

He's leaning on the door and squinting at me. The shack smells sour, as if someone threw up in there.

"Eddie Ferrari." I lean forward so Richie won't hear me. "Remember that rainy day. The shovel?"

"I don't have your damn shovel. Stop bothering me."

Jim staggers over and sits on the bed. The blanket is all bunched up, and there aren't any sheets, just the bare mattress.

"Are you sick, Jim?" I step inside.

"Never been sick a day in my life. Strong as an ox. I fought in the Great War. 'Over there,' " he starts singing. " 'Over there. Da-da-da, da-da-da, over there. Oh, the Yanks are coming, the tanks are coming' . . . ha, ha, ha, 'Tanks for the memory' . . . ha, ha, ha!"

Jim is like a different person. It's a little scary.

"You showed me your uniform," I remind him, "and told me about your sweetheart. In France?"

Jim looks at me real hard.

"Who'd you say you were?"

"Eddie Ferrari. You told me to come and see you again."

"I did? Don't remember."

I'm starting to feel embarrassed.

"How's Sunny?" I ask.

"What do you want with Sunny?" Jim starts to get up, but he can't. "He's the only friend I got. *Psss! Psss! Psss!* Come on, Sunny."

Sunny crawls out from under the bed and jumps into Jim's lap.

"Hello, buddy boy." Jim scratches the cat behind the ears. "You like that?"

Sunny rubs his head under Jim's chin, and for

a second Jim is the way he was last time. Then he scowls.

"You scared us, knocking on the door. Making me bump into the table. What are you doing here, anyway?"

"I just stopped by to say hello."

"Well, you said it. Now say 'Good-bye.' We don't like company, do we, Sunny? 'Oh, climb up on my knee, Sunny boy. . . .' " Jim is singing again. " 'Climb up on my knee, Sunny boy. . . .' "

"Good-bye, Jim," I say, and I walk out the door.

"I thought you were a goner." Richie comes running around from the other side of the shack. "I saw through the window. What were you talking about? Was he singing?"

I clear my throat and say, "It was all crazy stuff about when he was in the Army."

"He looked like he was drunk," Richie says. "Weren't you scared?"

"A little, but he's just a harmless old hermit, and hermits like to be left alone. We shouldn't bother him again."

"I never thought you'd really do it. I couldn't believe my eyes when you went inside."

"Come on, Richie. Let's go back to the clubhouse and let Neil out."

"You should have been there," Richie is telling

everybody. "Jim was rip-roaring drunk, and Eddie went right inside and talked to him."

"When Angel told me the double dare," Neil says to me, "I didn't think you could do it. I figured I'd be a prisoner forever."

"What'd you and Jim talk about?" Angel asks.

"He told me he didn't like anybody around except his cat."

"That big old tiger?" Peggy's voice quivers. "I wouldn't go near it."

"Me either." Mikey shakes his head.

"I thought Jim was going to sic him on you," Richie says.

"I don't think you can sic cats on people," Angel says. "Just dogs."

"Jim reminds me of the witch in 'Hansel and Gretel.' " Peggy grins.

"His shack should be made out of candy," Mikey says, and they all laugh.

"Let's pretend that I'm Jim the Hermit," Neil says, "and the clubhouse is my shack."

"I want to be the cat." Peggy does her fingers like claws. *"Meooooow!"*

"And I'll be"—Mikey stops to think—"the man from the draft board checking on Jim because he's not registered."

"That's no fun," Peggy says to her brother. "Can't you be somebody interesting?"

"I'll be President Roosevelt," Mikey replies.

"In Jim the Hermit's shack?" Peggy squeals.

They all giggle and go inside the clubhouse.

"I have to go." I start walking away. "I promised my father I'd weed the Victory garden."

"Angel," Richie says, "are you playing softball on Saturday?"

"Yes," my brother says.

"Want to come over to my house for some batting practice?"

"O.K."

"Hey, Eddie, you want to come?" Richie calls after me.

"I don't know." I stop to kick a pebble and notice my shoelace is untied.

"Come on," Angel coaxes. "You can weed the garden later. I'll help you."

"Well, I'm not too good at hitting." I tie my shoe.

"You'll never get good if you don't practice," Richie says. "Did you ever try pitching?"

That's a good idea. A lot of great baseball pitchers are lousy hitters.

"O.K.," I say, and we're off to the Egan house. I wonder if I'll get to go inside.

★ 13 ★

V-Mail

It's fall now, and I've been inside the Egan house lots of times.

"Summer sure went by fast. Didn't it, Duke?"

When he looks at me like that, I think it means he agrees.

I fold up the V-mail letter I just finished writing to Uncle Hugo. V-mail is a wartime invention to save paper. You write your letter on one side of the sheet, and then it folds so that the other side becomes the envelope. It's a very good idea, and I hope I'm folding it the right way. Uncle Hugo's address is a whole lot of numbers which are a code for where he is overseas. My father thinks it's North Africa. We know that he's a clerk in company headquarters, which is a little safer than being on the front lines, and he probably won't have to shoot at anybody. I never play with my BB gun anymore. Before I seal the letter, I decide to reread it to make sure I didn't misspell any words.

Dear Uncle Hugo,

How are you? We are all fine. School started 3 weeks ago and I'm in the 6th grade. I like my teacher. Her name is Mrs. Crosbie. Her husband is a sargent in the Army.

We had a lot of tomatoes from the Victory garden. My mother put some in jars for over the winter. Last week we were invited to the Molinas' for dinner. It was good. Mr. Molina said it was all imported olive oil and tomatoes and things that he bought from the black market. My father says we're not going there for dinner anymore.

We painted the clubhouse green. It looks nice but it's kind of crowded now. The Defense Club has three new members. This summer we made friends with some kids we used to fight with. Neil is the new treasurer and Gloria is still secretary. When her hair grew back a little, Mrs. Maloney took her to get a permanent at the beauty palor.

There's a War Bond Drive at school and the Defense Club is helping. We made posters to hang in the halls. Mrs. Crosbie is in charge of the Bond Drive and I'm her assistant.

The Cardinals shut out the Yankees 2 to 0 today in the World Series. That's the second straight game the Yankees lost. I have a 25¢ bet that the Cards win the Series.

We're going to Grandma's tomorrow. Uncle Ben and his new wife are going to be there. Dotty says

she has a Southern accent. I hope everything is
O.K. where you are. We miss you.

Your loving nephew,
Eddie

P.S. I gave my ball of tinfoil to the last Scrap Drive.

"Ma!" I yell up from the basement. "How do
you spell 'sergeant'?"

"S-E-R-G-E-A-N-T!" she yells down.

I cross out "sargent" and write "sergeant"
above it. I wish I could rewrite the whole letter
without any mistakes, but that would be wasting
paper.

"Ma! Is 'assistant' A-S-S-I-S-T-A-N-T?"

"That's correct!"

"Thanks!"

I fold the letter back up, seal it, and put a stamp
on it. After I come back from the mailbox, I'm
going to start working on the sign for Jim the
Hermit. On a nice piece of wood I'm going to
draw a picture of a sleeping cat and under it print
"DO NOT DISTURB." Jim can put it up on his
door so nobody will bother him. I want to give
it to him for Christmas.

"Come on, Duke. Let's go mail Uncle Hugo's
letter."

It's O.K. for Dukie to run loose in the empty

lots, but my father doesn't want him running on people's lawns. So I put his leash on him, and we run out through the garage.

"Where are you going, Eddie?" Richie Egan calls. He and Mikey and Peggy are in their front yard.

"To mail a letter to my uncle. Did you listen to the game?" I ask.

"Yeah, but don't think you're going to win the bet. The Yankees are only one game behind."

"Is that V-mail?" Mikey asks.

"Let me see," Peggy says.

I show them my letter.

"Want to walk me to the mailbox?"

"Can I hold the leash?" Peggy asks.

"Go ahead."

"Let's race," Mikey says. "Ready, on your mark, get set, go!"

We all run. Peggy lets go of Dukie's leash, and he gets to the mailbox first.

"Dukie won." She laughs.

"Good boy," I say and scratch Dukie behind the ears. He's panting and looks like he's smiling. The Egans and I are panting, too, and giggling.

"Are you going trick-or-treating with us?" Richie asks as we all walk back from the mailbox.

"Sure," I say.

"What's your costume?" Mikey wants to know.

"It's a secret," I tell him. "Don't you want to be surprised?"

"Want to know what we're going as?" Peggy is dying to tell.

"I think Halloween costumes should be kept secret," I say. "But if you want to tell, go ahead."

"I'm going as Betsy Ross," she says, "and I'll be sewing thirteen stars on the first flag. Richie and Mikey want to go as the *Spirit of '76*, but they need someone to be the little drummer boy."

"Don't look at me. I'm going as Uncle Sam," I break down and tell them. "I've already got the hat, the beard, the tailcoat, and everything."

"You told your secret." Peggy grins.

"Would Angel go as the little drummer boy?" Mike asks.

"I doubt it. He's going as"—I almost say who—"somebody else."

Angel is going as Mandrake the Magician, but that's his secret.

"What about Neil?" asks Mikey.

"Maybe." I know Neil doesn't have a costume yet. "Ask him."

"Is Angel's costume patriotic?" Richie has an idea. "Wouldn't it be terrific if the Defense Club all dressed patriotically?"

"It would," I agree. "But Angel's costume isn't."

"If Neil is the drummer boy," Richie plans, "maybe Gloria would go as the Statue of Liberty."

"With a peek-a-boo bang?" Mikey giggles.

We all laugh.

"Angel might change his mind when I tell him what everybody else is wearing," I say. "He might like going as George Washington."

"That would be great!" Richie sounds excited.

Then I get excited, too.

"And what about, if instead of just asking for candy and pennies, we asked people to pledge money for War Bonds or even sold them War Stamps?"

"That's the best idea yet," Richie says.

"I'll call a meeting of the Defense Club tomorrow," I decide.

"Want to come in and listen to *I Love A Mystery*?" Peggy asks when we get to the Egan house.

"I can't today." I take Dukie's leash from her. "I want to work on something I'm making. We'll have the meeting right after school tomorrow, O.K.?"

Richie, Mikey and Peggy all say, "O.K.," and go into their house.

"Come on, Duke," and we start to run.

Dukie grabs the leash with his mouth and growls his playful growl.

"You ought to be patriotic for Halloween, too," I say to him. "I'll ask Mrs. Crosbie if there were any famous dogs in American history."

I can't wait to tell her about selling War Bonds for Halloween. Maybe all the kids at school could do the same thing.

"That would be something important for the war effort, wouldn't it, Duke?"

I think Dukie agrees with me. His tail is wagging to beat the band.

About the Author

Edward Frascino grew up in Yonkers, New York, in an Albanian-Italian-American family much like Eddie Ferrari's. He also shared Eddie's earnest boyhood sense of patriotism during the years of the second World War. Today he says his concern extends further to include the well-being of the earth as a whole and the environment in which we live.

Ed Frascino's cartoons appear regularly in *The New Yorker,* and have recently been collected into a single volume, AVOCADO IS NOT YOUR COLOR. He has also illustrated many books for children, including THE TRUMPET OF THE SWAN by E. B. White, the Crystal books by Shirley Gordon, and his own EDDIE SPAGHETTI, to which this book is a sequel. He now lives in Brooklyn, New York, with his several wonderful cats.